Shoo Rayner

ROMAN
BRIT

GRIZZLY GLADIATOR

ORCHARD BOOKS
338 Euston Road, London NW1 3BH
Orchard Books Australia
Level 17/207 Kent Street, Sydney, NSW 2000

First published in 2015 by Orchard Books
ISBN 978 1 40833 454 6

Text © Shoo Rayner 2015
Illustrations © Shoo Rayner 2015

A CIP catalogue record for this book is available
from the British Library.

1 3 5 7 9 10 8 6 4 2

Printed in Great Britain

Orchard Books is an imprint of Hachette Children's Group and published by
The Watts Publishing Group Limited, an Hachette UK company.

www.hachette.co.uk

ROMAN BRIT

GRIZZLY GLADIATOR

ORCHARD

FORT FINIS TERRAE is a sleepy backwater in the great Roman Empire. A young shepherd boy named Brit lives there with his sheep and faithful dog Festus.

FORT FINIS TERRAE

INVERNIA

BRITTANICA

OCEANUS BRITTANICUS

GALLIA

EUROP

NOSTRU
MAR

AFRICA

ATLANTICUS
OCEANUS

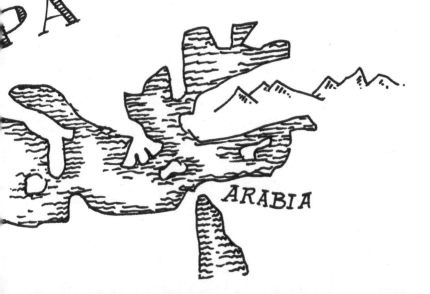

It's a quiet life for Brit and his animals in the fort. But every so often, something happens to make it a day to remember!

GERMANIA

PA

ARABIA

CHAPTER ONE

"As it's the Emperor's birthday," Drusilla trilled, "Daddy says I'm allowed to wear my new gold earrings. Aren't they gorgeous, Brit?"

Drusilla's father was the commander of Fort Finis Terrae, so Brit had to listen to her chatter. He wasn't her servant, but he wasn't really her friend either.

The two of them were sitting together outside Brit's barn, looking down over the hill.

Brit rolled his eyes. Who could be thinking about clothes and jewellery on this, the most exciting day of the year? It was the Emperor's birthday, and that meant the Circus was coming! Brit's tummy had been fluttering with anticipation all morning.

"They must be coming soon," said Brit, screwing up his eyes and staring into the distance. Something

on the far horizon caught his attention.

"Look! There they are!" he cheered.
"The Circus! It's coming!"

Drusilla squealed and tumbled
down the hill. Festus chased after her,
barking and scattering Brit's sheep in
all directions.

The Circus always came for the Emperor's birthday, but every year, no one dared to believe it until it had actually arrived and been set up outside the gates of Fort Finis Terrae. Anything might delay them – rain, mud, bandits, plague or just plain old laziness.

But here they were, back again, just as they had promised last year.

Brit's heart pounded with excitement as

he raced after Drusilla. The quiet summer's day exploded with the rattle of drums and the crash of cymbals. The air was filled with blaring, brassy trumpets.

Clowns led the procession, tumbling over each other, making the children shriek with laughter. The jugglers and stilt walkers, dressed in wild, colourful costumes, were followed by pony riders and the marching band.

In amongst them were the snake charmer, the fire-eaters and a magician, who made colourful handkerchiefs appear out of nowhere.

The children waved and cheered to their old friends. Festus snapped the air, trying to catch the magic handkerchiefs before they disappeared again.

At the back of the parade was a new attraction. A huge cage was roped onto the back of an ox cart. It was covered in curtains to conceal what lay inside. Festus growled and laid his ears flat.

"Do we have a treat for you tonight?" called the Circus Master to the gathering crowd.

"Oh my goodness, yes! Never seen in these parts before – a wild and terrifying beast, tamed only by ravishing beauty."

A beautiful young woman pulled back the curtains on the cart. Brit's eyeballs nearly popped as he peered through the bars and saw what was inside.

"ROOOOAAAAARRRRR!"

" Ladies, gentlemen, girls and boys, I give you Ursus, the Dancing Bear!" the Circus Master announced. "Come to the show tonight and see the terrifying creature dance for us."

Brit felt a thrill as Ursus shook the bars of his cage and roared. The crowd gasped and fell back. Festus hid behind Brit and whimpered.

Brit loved animals more than anything else. He was utterly transfixed – he'd never seen such a huge and powerful creature.

The bear met Brit's gaze. Ursus tilted his massive head with a quizzical look.

For a moment, the noise and excitement seemed to fall away. Then Ursus shook the bars and roared again.

"ROOOOAAAAARRRR!"

"You are magnificent!" Brit uttered under his breath.

CHAPTER TWO

Wanting to get closer to the bear, Brit busied himself helping the circus set up outside the gates of the fort. He noticed the beautiful young woman and the Circus Master arguing about something.

The woman stamped her foot. "I refuse to work with that stupid bear when he's in this mood!"

"But Angela!" the Circus Master pleaded. "You're the only one he will work with!"

"I don't care. Find someone else!" She tossed her head and stormed off angrily to her tent.

"But Angela!" the Circus Master cried again. "There is no one else!"

Brit cleared his throat loudly to get the Circus Master's attention.

"Maybe the bear's hungry," he suggested. "I could feed him for you? I love animals.

I'd do anything to get closer to him."

"If you like," the Circus Master grumbled. "But be careful…he's in a *very* bad mood."

Brit approached Ursus with a mixture of excitement and fear. The bear's collar was chained to a stake that was hammered into the ground. He growled like a bad-tempered old man.

Brit carried a basket full of carrots and loaves of stale honey bread. As he approached Ursus and offered the food, he whistled a tune he often used to calm his sheep.

Growling, with a deep, throaty rumble, Ursus took the bread in his huge paws. He never took his eyes off Brit as he ate.

Brit was fascinated. Ursus was enormous – and wild! Brit knew his sheep and goats well. They did what he wanted and went where he told them to go. Even Festus did what he was told – most of the time. But Ursus was different. No one would ever be his master.

Ursus licked his enormous lips and tried to stand up. He groaned and crashed down on his giant haunches.

Brit understood animals and straight away realised what the problem was.

"Poor thing!" he said. "You've got sore feet! No one can dance with sore feet!"

Brit thought for a moment.

"When my sheep get sore feet, I give them a special foot bath," he told Ursus. "Wait there. I'll be back soon."

Brit went for a walk, rummaging through the hedgerows, looking for the herbs and plants he used to keep his sheep healthy.

"Dandelion, marshmallow, horsetails and parsley," Brit muttered as he beat the plants to a pulp with a stick and swished the green mess around in a bucket.

Step by step, all the time whistling his calming tune, Brit crept up to the bear and offered him another loaf of honey bread.

Brit held his breath and slowly lifted up Ursus's giant feet. He placed them gently in the bucket of mush. "Here, let your feet soak in that for a while."

Ursus sighed a low growl of relief. He closed his eyes and almost seemed to smile.

It was amazing to be allowed to get so close to such a magnificent animal. Even though Brit wanted to plunge his fingers into the bear's thick, shaggy fur, he knew he had to be careful. Wild animals were not like pets – you never knew when they might turn on you and eat you up!

But Brit had lived with animals all his life. Somehow, he knew that Ursus trusted him.

"This will keep your feet nice and cool," he said. He carefully lifted the bear's giant paws out of the bucket, dried them and wrapped them in huge dock leaves.

"Where did you learn that?" asked the Circus Master, who had been watching Brit work his magic.

"I'm a shepherd," Brit explained. "I know about animals."

"You can help me get Ursus ready for the show tonight, if you like," said the Circus Master. "Even if Angela won't dance with him, the crowd will still want to see him."

CHAPTER THREE

The crowd of soldiers and their families
chattered excitedly as they waited for the
show to start. Drusilla and her family sat
in the special seats of honour.

"Behold, the Magnificent Ursus!"
the Circus Master proclaimed, as he
led the bear into the ring. "But alas,
we have no Beauty to tame the Beast.

Our lovely Angela is unable to dance tonight." The audience murmured their disappointment. They had not paid good money to stare at a grumpy old bear!

The muttering of the crowd died away as Drusilla marched out of her seat and into the circus ring. She stood with folded arms and tapped her new shiny sandals.

"I shall dance with the Beast!" Drusilla announced, her piercing voice cutting through the air like a butcher's knife. "I'm beautiful, aren't I, Daddy? Please, Daddy. Tell them I can!"

Gluteus Maximus, the Fort Commander, rose in his seat. "No one is more beautiful than you, my dear. I'm sure *you* can tame the Beast!" He never said no to Drusilla. She was a force of nature. Saying no to her was like trying to stop a thunderstorm!

Gluteus Maximus turned to the crowd. "We have a new Beauty," he announced. "The Beast WILL dance tonight!"

The audience cheered. Brit looked around at them, shaking his head.

They clearly thought Drusilla dancing with the bear was a great idea. They were probably hoping he would eat her!

Flaming torches lit up the faces of the crowd. Oil lamps flickered around the circus ring.

Drusilla marched right up to Ursus and waited for the music to start.

Brit could see from the Circus Master's face that he was worried. He was looking over at Drusilla's father, hoping  he would change his mind, but the Commander just smiled and waved to him to start the show.

The drums rolled…the cymbals crashed…the trumpets played a marching song and Drusilla pranced around the circus ring, waiting for Ursus to get up and dance with her.

"You show 'im, Drusy!" someone yelled from the cheap seats.

The crowd clapped and cheered, but Ursus merely swayed in time with the music. He was hypnotised by Drusilla's golden earrings that flashed with the beat. The shiny leaves of gold twinkled and glittered in the flickering light.

Ursus appeared to be in a trance. He hobbled towards Duscilla, grabbed her earrings and clipped them onto his furry ears. Drusilla watched, open-mouthed, as he twirled and flounced around the ring. The music made him feel light-headed and giddy.

The crowd roared their approval. It was all such fun.

"GIVE ME BACK MY EARRINGS!" Drusilla screamed.

The band stopped. The audience froze. Ursus stood still in shock. Brit rolled his eyes heavenwards. Drusilla was being Drusilla again!

Drusilla marched up to Ursus and stood in front of him, legs apart, hands on hips, eyebrows furrowed with anger and grim determination. "I SAID, GIVE ME BACK MY EARRINGS!"

Ursus looked down at the strange but fearless girl in front of him.

"I WANT THEM NOW!" Drusilla screamed. She lifted up her foot and brought the sharp edge of her heel down hard on the bear's left foot.

With a howl of pain, Ursus ripped his chain free from the wooden stake in the middle of the ring. The crowd panicked and fled in all directions, stumbling and tumbling over each other.

Ursus roared and raised his massive claws in the air. He swiped at the seats and benches, crushing them as if they were matchwood, then he crashed through the ring and lurched out into the darkness of the night.

Drusilla turned to the cowering crowd. "STOP THAT THIEF!" she screamed. "HE'S STOLEN MY NEW GOLD EARRINGS!"

At last, the soldiers had something to do. Picking themselves up from the floor, they grabbed flaming torches, raised their swords in the air and took up the chase.

"Stop, thief!" they whooped. "Kill that bear – he's a dangerous criminal!"

"Don't hurt him!" Brit called, running after them. "He didn't mean any harm!"

Festus was loving the commotion. He barked and howled and joined in with the sounds of panic and confusion.

"Come on, boy," Brit urged. "We've got to find Ursus before they do!"

CHAPTER FOUR

The full moon lit up the countryside with its pale, ghostly glow. The soldiers' flickering torches dotted the eerie landscape like fireflies. Their shouts and calls echoed across the fields, disturbing the peaceful summer night.

Festus ran about in all directions, sniffing the ground, seeking the bear's trail.

The scent had been trampled by fifty pairs of lumbering soldiers' sandals, but Brit's dog could still pick out the distinctive smell of the bear's feet, bathed in dandelion, marshmallow, horsetail and parsley juice.

Suddenly, Festus barked and made off in quite a different direction.

Brit followed. "You'd better not be chasing rabbits!" he called after him.

In the distance, Brit heard some of his sheep bleating with fear and panic.

Festus barked encouragement
to his master and crashed through the
scrub and undergrowth, towards the
sound. Brit followed, and they both
skidded to a halt when they saw the cause
of the commotion.

Ursus was lurching and stumbling
towards a tiny flock of sheep that was
trapped at the very edge of a flint quarry.

The quarry was a deep, chalky hole in
the ground, which

had provided the flint boulders that Fort Finis Terrae had been built with. It was very, very deep – if Brit's sheep fell into it, they could die!

Brit had to think quickly. "I'll try to distract Ursus," he whispered to Festus. "You go and save the sheep."

Brit's mouth was dry. He tried whistling his tune, but it was no good. He was still panting from all the running and his lips were parched.

He noticed that his feet were quite damp, though – a heavy dew had fallen earlier in the evening. Brit wiped his hand across the wet grass and put his fingers to his mouth. The water was instantly refreshing.

I hope there's no sheep poo on this grass! he thought.

Brit tried whistling again, and this time the tune was strong and clear. The haunting melody floated across the meadow.

Ursus stopped and slowly looked round. The sheep calmed at the familiar noise.

Festus quietly edged the flock of sheep away and led them to safety.

Ursus stood still on the edge of the quarry, watching Brit step closer and closer. As Brit continued to whistle his tune, the bear relaxed. His huge shoulders slumped. His legs gave way and he sat down with a thump on the grassy mound at the edge of the quarry.

Slowly, Brit reached and scratched
the bear between his giant ears.
Ursus closed his eyes
and sighed
a deep, rumbling
growl that Brit felt
vibrate through
the soft ground.

"There you
are, boy,"
Brit said.

Still whistling,
he unhooked
Drusilla's earrings
and put them safely in his pocket.

That's one problem solved, he told
himself.

Brit thought again about how much he loved animals. He stared up at Ursus again in wonder. He was truly magnificent! The great bear looked down at Brit, and the two of them stared at each other in silence.

The moment seemed to last for hours. Brit hardly dared to breathe.

Suddenly, the quiet, magical feeling was shattered by a shrill voice that seemed to ring down on them from the stars above.

"There he is! Kill him! Kill that bear. I want my earrings back!"

Ursus leaped to his feet again and roared with all his might.

Drusilla was charging towards them, like a barbarian on the rampage. A swarm of huge, hairy, hollering soldiers followed in her wake.

Ursus stamped and roared again. Brit felt his stomach lurch as the ground gave way beneath his feet.

Drusilla and the soldiers stopped dead, frozen like statues, as Brit and Ursus disappeared from view.

The grassy mound they'd been standing on had collapsed. Together, Brit and the bear tumbled down the side of the quarry wall and crashed into the hard, rocky floor below.

CHAPTER FIVE

"Arrrgh!"

"Raaaar!"

The bear's huge, hairy body cushioned the blow as Brit landed on top of him. Brit was alive, but the wind had been knocked right out of him!

I'm alive! Brit thought, as he fought desperately to breathe in.

He was covered in chalk dust. He spat and gasped for air at the same time.

He looked over at Ursus. Thank the gods! He was still alive too. Very slowly, dazed and confused, the bear began to pull himself up.

As the dust settled into the thin mist that swirled around the quarry floor, Ursus rose up to his full majestic height. Just like Brit, the bear was covered in chalk dust. He was as white as a ghost!

Brit was still struggling to breathe in – otherwise he would have gasped in amazement. Instead, a loud intake of breath from above made him look up.

Dotted along the edge of the quarry, soldiers were silhouetted against the moonlight. Their flaming torches reflected the fear in their eyes.

At last, Brit managed to gulp down a huge lungful of air.

At the same time, Ursus roared. But the bear was winded too, and his throat was full of chalk dust. The noise that came out of his mouth was an eerie, spine-tingling wail of pain, fear and rage.

Ursus was mesmerised by the
flickering lights of the soldiers' torches.
He staggered forwards and began to
climb. Just like the chalky walls of the
quarry, the bear's white, dusty body
glowed in the bright moonlight.

The soldiers were terrified. "It's a ghost!" they cried. "The bear's ghost has come back to haunt us! Quick – run for your lives!" The men fell over each other as they scrambled to get away.

But Drusilla was made of sterner stuff. She stood alone on the edge of the quarry, her shadow stretched across the ground.

 Another shape joined her. Festus peered over the edge and whimpered for his master.

"I don't care if you're a ghost or not!" Drusilla bellowed. "Give me back my earrings!"

Drusilla's shrieking seemed to reawaken some memories in Ursus. He cowered and whimpered, massaging his foot where Drusilla had stamped on it.

Brit wiped the chalk from his lips. The dust in his lungs and the echo from the quarry walls made Brit's voice sound as dry as the grave.

"Drusilla-silla-silla!" he called.

Drusilla saw Brit's ghostly form glow white in the moonlight. He seemed to rise out of the swirling mist as if he had just risen from the dead.

"Oh!" There was a tone of doubt in Drusilla's voice. Was this really Brit's ghost? Festus began howling for his dead master.

Brit raised a hand towards Drusilla, something golden flashing in his fingers.

"I've got-got-got your earrings-ings-ings!" he moaned in his dry, echoing voice. "Wait there-ere-ere. I'll bring them to you-oo-oo-ou!"

Drusilla turned and ran for her life. "Gho-o-o-o-o-o-sts!" she screamed.

The ground shook and the leaves on the trees trembled as she hurtled through the fortress gates, screaming to the guards to slam them shut and lock them behind her.

Brit gave a chuckle, which quickly turned into a chalky cough. He turned to Festus and the great bear and shrugged. "Come on," he said to them both. "Back to the land of the living."

CHAPTER SIX

The next day, after Brit had convinced everyone he was not a ghost, he showed Angela how to look after Ursus's feet. They put on another show that night, and it was a great success. Ursus did like dancing with Angela, and he loved the applause of the crowd. It was just the sore feet that had made him grumpy.

After the show, the Circus Master asked Brit to come away and join them on the road. Brit could hardly sleep that night for thinking of all the places he might go, the animals he might meet and the sights he might see.

But the next day, as the warm sun rose over his little part of the world, he remembered his sheep, and the goats and the chickens and Festus – they all needed him. He had to stay.

"It's a shame you can't come with us," sighed the Circus Master, as they said their goodbyes. "We could do with a bright young lad like you. I've never known anyone so good with animals."

Brit smiled, then he and Festus climbed to the top of the hill. They waved as they watched the Circus march down the road. Soon they were just a tiny dot on the horizon.

Drusilla appeared at his side. "Hello, Brit!" she said cheerily. "I thought I'd find you here. Would you like to see my new ring? Isn't it a beauty?"

Brit sighed. Here we go again, he thought. Back to listening to Drusilla drone on about clothes and jewellery. Maybe he should have left with the Circus after all? He leaped to his feet and stared into the distance.

But the Circus was long gone. Brit sighed again, and Festus pushed his cold, wet nose into his master's hand. He wagged his tail and looked up at Brit with big, baleful brown eyes.

"Oh, Festus," Brit smiled. "At least I can always talk to you!"

ROMAN
BRIT

COLLECT THEM ALL!